Groping in Darkness:

Between Talgarth and Hong Kong

黑暗中摸索：

塔爾加夫與香港之間

Sau Y. Chan

To :

Antonia, Jenni, Roy, Peter

&

In Memory of

Hilary Scott-Archer

March 2020

Prologue

Not only that none of the poems in the present collection has been published, I am also a "poet" who has never published any poem, though a number of my pieces were recited or sung in the meetings of Swans of Usk, the poetry group based in Brecon of mid-Wales, to which I belonged.

I wish to thank the late Hilary Scott-Archer and my good friend Peter Brooke for helping me through the revision of this collection; without them, it would not have come into existence. I am also indebted to my other friends Jenni Rule, Roy Powell, Antonia Spowers, Patricia Evans, Mike Scott-Archer, and Chris Meredith who have read or heard some of the drafts and have given me inspiring suggestions and encouragement, and to Amy who was always the first person to read the early drafts and to realise my poetic writings were worthwhile. Now looking back, it all started as an escapade.

Other than being my good friends, Jenni, Roy and Peter have been my poetry tutors, Antonia was our former neighbour and one of our first friends in Talgarth who always took care of us, cooked us good meals, allowing us to share her bathroom whenever we had a boiler problem, reading my manuscripts, and introducing her friends to us. And Mike and Hilary were generous hosts of our poetry group meetings.

Being a non-native speaker of English, a Chinese born and raised in Hong Kong and educated in the United States, and a resident of Wales from January 2008 to May 2015, I somehow find my adventure in English poetry a most fascinating experience. I suppose the rich legacy of Chinese poetry which I have inherited, and the Welsh bardic tradition that I was exposed to have certainly played a part in forging my creative urges. Now looking back, it all started as an escapade.

I would also thank my friend Chor Koon-fai for the translation of 5 of my English pieces into Chinese. Above all, I must offer my heartfelt gratitude to Peter Jay who has edited and commented on 5 of the most favourite pieces of my own. Also, my thanks to Suk Lee who introduced Mr Jay to me.

The present collection contains 60 poems written from 2011 to 2019, 15 in Chinese and 45 in English. Also there are my English translation of 7 classical and contemporary Chinese poems, and Mr Chor's Chinese translation of 5 of my English pieces.

May I thank all those friends and people who have posed, though inadvertently, for my portrayal.

SYC
Hong Kong

Contents

1. Graveyard

11th December 2012,
Revised 12th August and 4th July 2016

Here lie women with their little secrets,
Men and their daring tales.
Under the sculpture, plinths and masonry,
Are yesterday's winners and heroes.

The headstones are icy cold,
Whether they are dry or bedewed.
Some proudly stand straight,
A few solemnly tilt.
While your eyes turn away,
One shifts its angle in stealth.

Some playfully blur their inscriptions
With a thin cobwebby curtain
Raised by impish Angels
Who can't restrain their giggles.
While you rub your eyes,
Quietly they scatter and gambol.

Buried too are the fantasies of boys and girls,
And infants' mumbles and gabbles.

Glistening in the air are the shards
Of their parents' broken hearts.
The everlasting mist is the vapour
Of all their tears and expectations.

Look! Husbands have become canopies,
Wives are their leaves.
Daughters wear petals of all colours,
Sons make the weeds and grass.
In fact they haven't died,
This is the place of new lives!

Appendix

墓地
Graveyard

左冠輝譯

這裏躺著帶同小秘密的婦女、
男子漢和他們的勇猛故事。
雕像、座基和磚石之下，
是昨天的勝利者和英雄。

墓碑雪冷如冰，
乾或露濕時都一樣。
有些傲然直立，
有幾塊肅穆地傾斜。
你望向別處時，
有一塊偷偷把角度移換。

有些逗玩地隱沒碑文，
調皮的天使
掀起蛛網帷幕時，
也忍不住咯咯地笑。
你揉眼睛的一剎那，
她們靜靜蹦跳四散。

埋藏的還有少男、少女的幻想，
以及幼孩的咿咿呀呀。
空中閃閃發光的碎片，
是他們父母傷碎了的心。
那常年不散的水氣，
是他們眼淚和期望的霧化。

看啊！丈夫變成樹冠，
妻子是上面的綠葉。
女兒戴著五顏六色的花朵，
兒子化作莠草和綠茵。
他們其實沒有死亡，
這裏是新生的地方！

2. Carol of Blaenavon

17th July 2012,
revised 1st August 2014, 8th October 2014

She smiles to strangers,
Hands tea to the hungry,
Extending her hours for soaked travellers,
Offering warmth to the cold.

Our country, she says, was not of wars and battles
But also of slavery, defeats and conquests.
Our fathers bled in farms, mines and mills,
Our mothers dug peat for heat.

Not just of castles and princes was our land,
But also of labour and inequality.
Ironwork Hall is round the corner,
Not far away is Big Coal Pit.

Wales is about bards, dances and eisteddfods,
Also of idleness and intolerance.
Hard work is a powerful word,
Equality a Welsh ambition.

When she talks to her guests
She pays equal attention to everyone,
Not assuming anyone is worthless
Or he or she doesn't know anything.

She appreciates people as individuals,
Never presuming one is rude
Or doesn't know her language
Because of a different complexion.

The barrier is not how we look or speak,
But is built of vanity and sloth.
Those remnants of colonial days
Are culprits of prejudice and bigotry.

It brings neighbours and wayfarers together,
Her café is a meeting place.
Feeding them, knowing them, is her pride,
Her door is never shut to anyone.

She runs a winning venture,
Always giving before she takes.
Carol doesn't do it for the pennies,
Her business is to save the world.

We met Carol on 16[th]July, my birthday.

Appendix

布萊納文的卡蘿
Carol of Blaenavon

左冠輝譯

她對陌生人微笑，
奉茶點給飢餓的人，
為濕透的旅客延長服務時間，
令寒冷的人感受她的溫暖。

我們的國家，她說，過去不只有大小戰爭，
也有奴役、戰敗和被征服。
我們的父親在農場、礦洞和磨坊裏淌血，
我們的母親靠掘泥煤取暖。

我們的土地過去不只有城堡和王子，
也有勞動和不平等。
鐵工會所就在轉角，
不遠處就是大煤坑。

威爾斯確有吟游詩人、舞蹈和詩歌比賽，
也有閒散和執著。
勤勉是有力的字眼，
平等是威爾斯的志向。

她和客人說話時
不會忽視任何人，
不會假定某人冇用
或者某人甚麼都不懂。

她欣賞的都是獨立個體，
從不假定不同膚色的人
必然無禮
或者不懂她的語言。

隔閡不由我們的外貌和說話造成，
全因自大和怠惰。
殖民地時代的殘渣
是歧視和唯我獨尊的禍首。

集鄰居與旅人在一起，
她的咖啡館是相逢的地方。
她以餵飽、認識他們為榮，
門總是為所有人打開。

她的營運所向無敵，
在取得之前一直首先付出。
卡蘿不是為錢而做，
她的生意是挽救這個世界。

我們在 7 月 16 日巧遇卡蘿，那天是我的生日。

3. Janet Dancing in Silence

26th July 2012,
revised 24th November 2013, 9th October 2014

Whenever she wishes,
Everything moves on, but stops making sound.
She feels the earth's pulse with her feet,
Twirling in the rhythm of air.

An ethereal tune reverberates in her veins
Driving her to swiftly cast.
A kiss-curl drops from her long, pleated hair,
Rippling along with her billowing flimsy dress.

Brightness is brilliance in perfect peace,
In sheer silence heat becomes hilarity.
On a streak of thermal she steps,
To a stir of wind she swirls.

Ponies and donkeys are in her mind,
Together with parrots large and small.
If they can dance and sing without music,
She can do everything without a sound.

Then, at her additional request,
Gravity is undone.
There she skips, takes off,
And away the girl flies.

Janet is an elegant dancer who has not been hearing since childhood.

4. On Her Return

12th November 2012,
revised 30th November 2012

Dear Antonia, Jenni and Roy:
At last Amy has come back
To our home in Hong Kong
From the faraway Talgarth we also call home.

She has completed a trip of wind and rain
From seeing you painters, writers,
Dancers and visionaries,
Poets, sculptors, singers and dreamers.

Four years of amity
Has opened a world to us.
Thank you for those warmest moments of our lives
When we were groping for love.

Take care, our friends,
Let nothing trouble your health.
Winter will soon be over,
Amy and I will return together.

When sprouts of spring will bud
In the mist we shall tightly hug.
Seeing each other again
Is the best gift we shall ever gain.

5. 往事如煙

2018 年 2 月 2 日

清香一炷，
插在爸媽相片前面，
浮煙繞繞。
凝視著他倆的寬容笑面，
重溫從前光景，
深吸那熟透氣味，
恍如昨天。

每個節日的早晨，
懶洋洋躺在牀上，
眼未張，
聞到了，
是媽向神靈點燃，
祈求保佑我們。
青煙裏，
洋溢無限溫暖。

轉眼一過近四十年，
搬回老家居住，
爸媽已仙遊十載，
如煙往事，

不堪回首。
借清香一枝，
我謹祝願：
他倆在天常為比翼鳥，
有來生，
我們重聚在
香煙繞繞！

6. Dear Ma and Ba

11th October 2014

My parents are old-timers
Who dislike emails and computers.
And as they have changed their way of life
They have cut off their phone line.
Now I can only tell them about us
By writing to them once in a while.

Dear Ma and Ba,
Amy and I are fine.
She now dances and sings on Mondays,
Rehearses with her choir on Thursdays,
Teaches piano on Fridays.
Plus the routine household chores
And the persistent writing of her diaries,
You can imagine she is not only fully occupied
But working towards something to which she aspires.

I have finished my novel on Alice
Whom you looked after
During her last few years.
Right now an editor is giving it a final touch
Before I again send proposals to agents.
It'll become a good book, I'm sure,

Except they don't think I'm good enough.
Currently I suffer from a crisis of confidence,
As I've been rejected five times already.

I've also been writing poems,
And translating verses from Chinese.
I hope they will form a collection
To be submitted to a contest.
For sure there are many better poets,
I take it as a challenge
For a beginner
Who has something to share.

Amy and I believe
We've missed the age
Where we could be good parents.
We have reached a consent
Of not having any children.
I know this will upset you,
Because it means our lineage will end.
Hopefully this will improve things
As we'll have a simpler world.

In a few months' time
We'll have lived here for seven years,
You'll have stayed there for eight,
Ma will be eighty-four,
Ba will be eighty-six.

We have made a number of good friends
Though others still regard us as sojourners.
I'm afraid it will take some time
Before they accept Orientals as equals.

I hope you have put behind
That legal case of some years ago.
I still think the court owes me an apology,
For I was reduced from witness to accused,
Was not even allowed a self defence.
I've never minded those lies they told to defame,
Except they probably broke your hearts.
I did it for justice,
And for honouring other witnesses' bravery.
Righteousness is the value I inherited from Ba,
Who told me to stand for it without fear.
Sometimes I regret I was abused by the media
Which forced me to bear the brunt.
But I have learnt the merit of forgiveness,
Just wish everyone will forgive and forget.

I'll travel to Hong Kong in late November,
Looking forward to revisiting our old family flat
Where you both had sweated
And shed tears bringing us all up.
I call second sister once a week, but
I haven't seen my eldest sister for some years,
I hope her problems will soon be overcome.

I am sharing with you a piece of good news:
With the help of herbal medicine,
My hypertension has been loosening.
I pass no single day without thinking of you,
Only I'm pleased to know you are together.
Have you seen grandpa and grandma recently?
How are my grandparents in River Pa?

Having finished this long overdue letter,
I shall place it in a metallic tub.
Writing it in Chinese or English makes no difference
Because thoughts transcend language.
Over fire I will entrust it to the wind,
Over the oceans will the ashes fly in the air,
To deliver to you
My words, love and tears.

Written at Strand, our village café in Talgarth.

Appendix

親愛的媽和爸
Dear Ma and Ba

左冠輝譯

我的父母是老派人，
不喜歡電郵、不喜歡電腦，
自從改變了生活方式後，
電話線也截了。
現在和他們談近況
只能偶爾給他們寫信。

親愛的媽和爸：
琬琪和我都很好。
現在她星期一跳舞和唱歌，
星期二到合唱團排練，
星期五教琴，
還有做日常的家務
以及持之有恆的寫日記，
你們可以想像她不但生活過得充實
而且還在努力追尋夢想。

寶鈿的小說我寫完了
在你們的照顧下
她渡過人生最後的幾年。

文稿正由一位編輯潤飾
然後我會再投稿給那些經理人。
我敢說這會是一本好書，
只是他們認為我不夠好。
最惱人是現在信心動搖，
畢竟曾經被五次退稿。

我也在寫詩，
還把中詩譯成英文。
我希望把作品輯成集子
拿去參加比賽。
當然比我好的詩人多得很，
我只當作是
想與人分享感受的
新手的磨鍊。

琬琪和我都覺得
我們已經過了
做稱職父母的年紀。
我們一致同意
不要生兒育女。
我知道你們會不開心，
為的是我們這房人就到此為止。
但願這樣做能把周圍改善，
因為我們的世界將會簡單一些。

再過幾個月
我們便在這裏住滿七年，
你們在那兒也八年了，
媽將會八十四歲，
爸八十六。
我們交了不少好朋友，
雖然其他人仍然當我們是過客。
我看恐怕要花點時間，
他們才會把東方人看待平等。

我希望你們不再耿耿於懷
幾年前那宗官司。
我仍然覺得法庭欠我道歉，
因為我由證人淪為被告，
即連自辯的機會也沒有。
我從來不把他們的謊言詆毀放在心裏，
但你們的心可能傷透。
我那樣做是為了公義，
也為了對其他證人的勇氣表示敬意。
正義感是我遺傳自爸的，
你教我伸張正義便不要懼怕。
有時候想起傳媒的報道便感到失望，
我被迫首當其衝承受攻擊。
不過寬恕的美德我明白了，
但願每個人都會寬恕和不記恨。

十一月尾我會去香港，
翹首以待重訪我們的老家，
在那裏你們曾流著汗、
也流著淚撫養我們成人。
我每星期找二姊一次，
但大姊已經好幾年沒有見面，
希望她的毛病很快可以治癒。

有好消息要告訴你們：
吃了草藥，
我的緊張情緒已漸漸舒緩。
我沒有一天不在想念你們，
唯一安慰的是你們已在一起。
最近有沒有見到爺爺和嫲嫲？
外公、外婆在琶江口可安好？

早已應該寫的這封信終於寫完，
我會把它放進鐵桶。
用中文或英文寫分別不大，
反正思念超越語文。
烈火裏我把信付託與風，
空氣裏飛灰越過重洋，
向你們送上
我的字、愛和淚。

寫於塔爾加夫我們村裏的小咖啡店「水濱」

7. Summer Daydream

31st May 2013

Never will I forget
That fine breezy *ha yet* – summer day.
You stood before the bright sun,
I couldn't see your bright face.

Your fluttering translucent dress
Was totally melting away.
The silhouette of a curvaceous body
Was all I could appreciate.

Lie down by my side, please,
Under the shade on the grass – *cou dei*.
Yet you lingered on the knoll
Bathing in the fiery rays.

There I closed my eyes,
Dreaming of on your lap I laid,
Softly stroking myself
As if I were touching you – *nei*.

A little piece composed some 40 years ago after a trip to
Stanley; originally in Chinese.

8. Crying Reaper

24th August 2012

The cold is closing in
As if it will strike at any time.
Darkness is drawing near
To the fields
Enshrouded by the clouds.

The barley a while ago
Was gilded and spoiled by the sun,
Now it is being mown down
Row after row.

The scene is nothing unfamiliar,
The seasons recur in a cycle.
The tired reaper carries a scarred heart,
Running his tractor hours after nightfall.

Rain has descended to his valley,
Love has lost its way on his land.
Why some choose to live for hatred?
Could they try to forgive?

He wears wrinkles and lines
Marked deep by

A life of hard work.
His brow is tightened,
His eyes glassy and unseeing.

There is no secret
In this part of the country.
He knows all his neighbours
Have been talking about his story.

Why some live for the past,
Selecting the bitter moments to remember?
Why they sow the wind
Still expecting apples in harvest?

Caught by the downpour
To which the drizzle has given place,
A big man like him has not cried
Since he was a little child.

Amidst the diary of a dead daughter
Telling how she was mistreated by her stepmother,
And her unforgiving sister
Who told her father to choose
Between her and his beloved partner,
Rob is caught in the whirlwind that howls.

9. 失去的妳

2017 年 12 月 5 日，2018 年 3 月 5 日

假如已發生的痛苦
能在我眼角續步後退，
之後加速褪色，
如列車駛離月臺，
把我載到下一站，
叫我兩眼前望，
在人群中
尋找愛我的人，
那便是生命殘酷後的恩賜。
假如天地不仁、
天昏地暗，
我還須豎起耳朵聆聽、
伸手摸索。

妳問我為何心如刀割，
是因失去了妳？
不啊，
是因妳逃避我的目光，
是因妳言不由衷，
是因妳擺佈我作代罪羔羊。

我告訴自己，
已給我的，
已是最好，
就把我們未完的一切，
留給命運、緣份。

答應妳，
我會常懷赤子之心，
毋忘初衷、
毋畏毋懼、
繼續獨自摸索。
於更闌人靜時，
我會思念不能是妳的妳、
妳那失去的妳、
我那失去的妳，
並在夢境裏
誠心為妳獻上
我的禱告！

10. Antonia

2nd August 2012, revised October 2014

Appalling, horrible, pathetic!
The world is dull and rotting!
Running out of energy,
It can't go on like this!
Why everyone is settling for second best?

Preposterous, ludicrous, ridiculous!
Poor Mother Nature must be defied.
Why should I go to bed?
What's wrong if I'm a hyperactive,
Restless septuagenarian?

Singlehandedly I drive
Two hundred miles for an exhibition.
My strong arms are holding up three sons,
Keeping eight grandchildren amused,
Bringing together admirers and friends.

Repeatedly I demonstrate to them:
Be whatever you want to be.
Marvellous, wonderful, extraordinary!
Persistence will free you from regrets,
Without passion life is what a waste!

I don't just put together things
That don't normally belong to each other.
I also create objects from nothing,
Which make you think twice and thrice
The meaning of existence.

I don't just cherish our family's noble flair,
I pass it on to my boys and girls.
Flouting space and time is my mission,
Sparking lightning is my ambition!
Why can't I?

11. Bright Stars of Talgarth

25th July 2011

Glittering and twinkling,
Way far up in the cold.
Beyond the drifting mist,
Above Black Mountains and Dinas Castle.

Over the barley, hedges and meadows,
They sparkle since time immemorial,
Filling up the immense space,
Comforting the sheep and cattle.

Halt and behold!
Because they might burrow
Deep into the clouds or haze,
Or be dimmed by the moon's glow.

They quietly dangle,
But not without an echo,
Piercing into our ears
When our eyes are closed.

In their depth something is glistening,
Ah, they are my fantasies, forgotten,

Projected upwards by a child,
In his countless nights of watching the sky.

Would you lift my marbles
To fly about and run wild?
Would you free me from the muddle
That makes me wail?

The clouds are coming in,
But please don't go
Before I retrieve my childhood dreams,
Before they bury this lonely one below.
Dear bright stars of Talgarth!
Oh!

12. High Street in a Welsh Village

Summer 2012

The *Welsh Girl* fails to attract admiring eyes,
Dylan Thomas is crouching in the corner.
Languishing in the dust covering them,
They wonder where have their lovers gone?

The unicorn is dozing in the hotel,
No one can tell whether it is open.
Along the street every window is longing
For their good old friends to come.

Once packed with lives and glories,
Now where is the missing energy?
Who will uncover its secret charm
And restore its lost beauty?

Have people been drawn towards
The mega malls' glamour and clamour?
Have some drifted away
Because of the town's grim past?

Even the bards are nowhere to be seen,

Who perhaps are overwhelmed by sadness.
Or perhaps they choose to stay indifferent,
Watching their home village fading in silence.

How brave are those who remain!
Running unwanted places,
Selling the same things but deemed unfashionable.
Nobody can guess how lonely they feel,
Except the one who has written a novel
But ruled unpublishable.

13. The Smallest Room

6th November 2014, revised 10th March 2015

Hiding it in a corner,
No owner ever takes pride in it.
It is placed at the farthest end,
Beyond long, narrow corridors.

Its door is obscure,
Opening into an unheated area.
Rarely is anyone there,
Except those appearing in the mirrors.

It is badly lit,
Making it unbelievably dark.
Very often I've to grope my way in,
Losing my way out is not unusual.

No one wants to linger there,
Darting off even before they're done.
Many don't even wash their hands,
As if afraid of being caught by the taps.

The mirrors on the wall
Are usually dusty and cloudy.

Whenever I look deep into one
I find myself rendered different.

Sometimes I see myself older, frailer,
Bearing new lines I've never discovered,
Or resembling a person I've never met.
Once I doubted if I was wearing those rags.

Gnomes and puzzles might appear,
Hinting at something no one can decode.
Every time I've figured out the answer,
The lines have re-phrased themselves.

It is often very quiet,
But a drip of water can be sudden and loud,
Sonorously ricocheting on the walls
Scaring those who over focusing
On their own water spouts.

Some declare themselves to be ancient,
Sounding the silence of centuries ago,
Exuding a smell a millennium old,
Whisking you back in time
In a split second.

There is always an inner cubicle,
Few dare give it even a look.
It doesn't seem like it's unoccupied

Though you can't see any shoes or legs.

It is labelled by a pair of moustaches,
A figure with sprawling limbs,
Or a top hat with or without a walking stick.
It has nothing to do with J.S. Bach
It is the uncanny shadowlands
They call Ty Bach.

Appendix

最小的房間
The Smallest Room

左冠輝譯

把它藏在角落，
沒有主人會因它感覺光彩。
它處於最遠的一端，
在長而狹窄的走廊之後。

遮掩隱蔽的門，
打開進去是冰冷的地方。
在內難得會見到人，
除了鏡子裏出現的面孔。

裏面燈光非常不足，
難以置信可以這樣陰暗。
我往往須摸索進去，
出來時迷路常常。

誰也不要在裏面逗留，
辦完事便奪門而出。
很多人甚至手也不洗，
像是害怕被龍頭一把抓著。

牆上的鏡子
通常都塵封及朦朧不清，
每次我找一面仔細去看，
發覺自己變了另一個模樣。

有時看到自己蒼老、虛弱，
多了些縐紋一直沒有察覺，
或者像一個從不認識的人，
甚至驚見竟然穿著那些破衣。

牆上或會貼起謎語、雋句，
卻沒有人會知意何所指。
每次我想到答案，
驚見它的句子已作改動。

這裏常常寂寂無聲，
但一滴水可以突然響起，
聲音在四壁迴盪，
出其不意嚇驚那些
過份專注自己水柱的人。

有些自稱歲月久遠，
幾世紀前的靜邃今天可聽，
千年古味緩緩可聞，
把你送回舊時
於一瞬之間。

總會有最內裏的間隔，
鮮有人鼓勇氣瞥它一眼。
似乎那兒並非無人，
雖然你看不到鞋子或腳。

它標記著一對八字鬍子、
攤開四肢的人形、
或者高頂禮帽、連或不連手杖。
和約翰巴赫半點關係也沒有，
這神秘古怪的幻境，
大家稱之為「替巴赫」。

威爾斯語 Ty Bach 指洗手間，音譯「替巴赫」；約翰巴赫 (J.S.
Bach) 是十八世紀德國大音樂家。

14. 海玻璃女孩

2018 年 2 月 21-25 日

是海浪抑或誰人曾把瓶子打碎？
是何故、何時、何日？
誰說沙灘上歲月從不留痕？
碎片上不就刻劃了
波濤的擊打、沙粒的洗擦？
每片都得著
語言無從描繪的形態。
從前的通透，
今天是肉眼無法窺破的迷宮。
若說分離、散落是因命運，
偶遇、相聚便是緣份。

我叫妳把它們帶回家去，
養在清水、玻璃杯裏，
看有形與無形的對比，
想像前緣與後果、
破碎與團聚，
感受無聲的歲月
如疾風在我們指間吹過。
我還要妳答應
一年後送它們回歸自然，

因為借來的，
我們無權佔有。

日在遠方漸落，
我和妳爬上懸崖邊的矮牆，
神氣地讓妳媽咪拍照。
妳把手搭在我的膊上，
我把妳摟進臂彎。
無緣中的有緣、
偶遇中的相聚。
亭亭玉立、
一頭長髮、
一臉稚氣、
不畏欠缺中向前望，
無人能看透才十六歲的妳，
卻在我眼中
是長得何樣漂亮、完美！

15. Mayhem

25th August 2014

"No! Wrong hands!"
Yells the Master
As soon as he commences
The first dance of the class.

"The Ones are improper!"
Cries the Master
Who sees most of his men
Line up in disorder.

Startled by the Master
They raise their right hands
In their desperate attempt
To form a left-hand star.

"Keep going with your partner!"
He calls louder and louder
Because the coming circle
Looks absolutely disastrous.
Some have only turned a half,
A few have moved too fast,
Others just assume

It's one and a quarter.

When he points to the "right,"
To the left some cast.
Others keep on reeling
When he bids them to pass.
Then he says "step back,"
But a few go forward instead.

The double figure of eight
Is not any better
Because some confused men
Wouldn't separate from their pairs.
Their women are left behind
To bump into each other.

The poor Hay-In-A-Mirror
Is a total failure
As the dancers have no idea
When to go around,
When to dance straight
Right through the centre.

At last the Master's grumbling
Gives way to a puzzle,
As if he has seen
An unbelievable miracle:
When the dance draws to a close,

All the dancers have arrived at
Exactly the positions
They have been expected to go.

As if all of that
Isn't a big upset,
The Master just figures out
Another important fact:
Of the three instruction sheets,
One had given him the slip,
And has been hiding somewhere,
In truth, under his seat!

As if all of these
Are nothing indeed,
The Master takes a look
At the title of the piece.
He finds it exactly reads
"Mayhem"!

For Jenni's birthday.

16. Echo My Words

16th October 2014, revised 4th July 2016

Gradually and unnoticeably
Night's curtain has lowered itself.
Outside the windows of the café
Tall posts holding the veil of bluish-grey,
The street faintly lit up by the lamps.

Today is the sixteenth of October,
This moment seven-thirty pm,
More than half of the day has gone.
Amy is with her choir - or with someone else,
I'm here to write my poem.

More than half of my life has gone!
Gradually and unnoticeably
Sickness and loneliness are looming upon.
I wonder how much more time I'll have,
For whom am I putting together these lines?

I don't have children,
I'll never make a great poet,
Porky and Goosey don't read an alphabet!
It's for Amy that I write

Who might read it one day when she looks back.

No, it doesn't really matter
Whether she'll relive our past or not.
In fact I'm creating a dialogue
Between myself and the still world:
Stones, tarmac and walls never speak,
They just echo my words.

Written at Strand, Talgarth.

Appendix

迴響我的說話
Echo My Words

左冠輝譯

漸漸的、不經不覺地，
夜幕已低低垂下。
咖啡店的窗外，
高柱支撐起灰藍色的紗帳，
燈光把街道隱約照亮。

今天是十月十六日，
此際是晚上七時三十，
一天已過去不止一半，
妻子正和她的合唱團或者某人一起，
我在這裏寫我的詩。

過了不止一半的也是我的生命！
漸漸的、不經不覺地，
病痛和寂寞迫人而來。
我不知道自己還有多少日子，
這些詩句又究竟為誰沉吟？

我沒有兒女，
永遠不會成為大詩人，

笨豬和獃鵝根本目不識丁！
我是為妻子而寫，
或許一天她回望時會讀到。

不，她會否重溫從前光景，
根本無關痛癢。
其實我是與靜默的世界對答：
石塊、柏油路和牆壁從來無言，
只迴響我的說話。

寫於塔爾加夫的「水濱」

17. In that Remote and Distant Place

Translated, 26th July 2014

In that remote and distant place,
There is a lovely maid.
Whoever passes by her tent
Always turns back to linger and gaze.

Her dainty, rosy cheeks,
Glows like the red sunrays.
Her beautiful charming eyes
Glitter as bright as the moon's rage.

I will give up all I have,
Follow her to walk her sheep.
Daily admiring her smiling face,
Her pretty golden clothes I'll praise.

I wish to become a little lamb,
By her side I'll stay.
I long to feel her soft whip
Brushing against me tenderly all the way.

Translated from a song written by Wang Luo-bin (1913-1996) in
1939; intended to be sung in English.

Appendix

在那遙遠的地方
In that Remote and Distant Place

王洛賓（1913-1996）

在那遙遠的地方，
有位好姑娘，
人們走過了她的帳房，
都要回頭留戀地張望。

她那粉紅的小臉，
好像紅太陽，
她那美麗動人的眼睛，
好像晚上明媚的月亮。

我願拋棄了財產，
跟她去放羊，
每天看著那粉紅的小臉，
和那美麗金邊的衣裳。

我願做一隻小羊，
跟在她身旁，
我願她拿著細細的皮鞭，
不斷輕輕打在我身上。

18. See You Next Life

6th - 7th August 2014

Every time I see you boarding the bus to Cardiff,
No tears, no sighs, no sorrow,
To me you bid "See you soon,"
To you I say "See you next life."
We'll stay apart until your return,
Live together before the next separation.
Then either you will send me off
Or I'll see you leave.

Every night sitting on the edge of my side of our bed,
You sing me a lullaby and say "Goodnight,"
I reply with my favourite line.
Every time I go for a jog
Or for an errand in town,
I say "See you next life."
Life is composed of endless journeys:
A sleep, like a jog, is a trip,
There are chances we'll never again meet.

A joke remains a joke until that moment:
You will see me depart for my last travel,
Or on your eternal trip I'll see you embark.

Tears might downpour like torrents,
Thousands of words get choked at our throats,
Or we'd stay calm and silent,
Except to chorus,
"See you next life."

After my body has died
I am reduced to a shadow
Not more than half of what I used to be.
I stay with you for a long while,
Trying to follow you close,
But as I further lose my strength,
I easily drift away
Like a helpless child,
For a day, a month or for a long, long time.

Gradually you no longer feel me roaming in our house,
Touching your wrist to soften the brushing of your teeth,
Sitting next to you in our car,
Nagging you to keep a distance from the curb,
Tightening the screws of your glasses,
Or tickling Porky and Goosey to make them shudder.
You lose the tiny movements of my breathing,
The scent of me,
My weight on the mattress,
As I keep losing myself
And the consciousness of you,
But drifting

Far, faraway.

One day,
While my ultra transparent and ever fading self
Is seated on a bench by the road,
I see a woman of silvery long hair and serenity,
Hobbling with a cane
Towards a corner store.
It wakens the last remains of my soul,
Telling me it is you.

My sight of you
Prompts your recognition of my presence.
Your sweet smile all of a sudden
Succumbs to a sob.
You recall all our sweetest moments
Every one of which brings you tears like rains.
Without knowing where I am,
You fetch Porky and Goosey from the car
Waving them in the air,
Urging me to go home
Vowing we will never again part.

I try to cling to you,
But I fail to do as you wish,
For I am too feeble
To be able to attach to anything,
Or to give you my touch,

As if in any split second
I'm about to totally decompose.

Perhaps countless years have elapsed since my death,
You've lost count of the Olympic Games' come and go.
At this critical instant,
All I can do is to mouth,
See you next life.

For our 14th and very last anniversary.

19. Lullaby for Jenni's Birthday

25th August 2012

Jenni, sleep, Jenni,
Roses have been waiting
To creep through the window,
To reaching your arms,
Snuggling in your rosy palms.

Jenni, sleep well, Jenni,
Squirrels, rabbits, mice will gather around
When morning dawns in no time.
They'll croon, lilt and celebrate
Every day is your birthday.

Sleep, Jenni, sleep,
Raccoon will sing Robert Burns' song
When you open your eyes.
He'll reel like the Exciseman and De'il,
Just to make you roll about in the aisles.

Jenni, Jenni, sleep, sleep,
Close your eyes now.
Tomorrow will just be fine.

We shall deal bravely
With problems that arise.

Jenni, sleep well, Jenni,
No more worries.
Put aside the uncertainties,
Little animals will nibble away at the hurdles,
Tomorrow a fresh start will unfold.

20. 過客

2017 年 12 月 19 日

妳不再回答我的訊息，
正是別一種的回應。
我的名字
在妳電話裏無窮後退，
我在妳身邊溜走。
心碎，
淚如泉湧，
慚愧一度
入侵妳的世界。

即使擦身而過，
何嘗不是緣份？
離地的傾情，
卻絕無非份之想。
但我無權令妳煩惱，
無權要求妳、
無權想念妳，
只能君子地
目送妳的冰肌玉骨
乘風歸去。

知妳捱更抵夜，
曾使我暗地神傷。
叫妳保重嬌軀，
因為妳嬌如黛玉。
妳是丈夫的寵妻、
小天使的俏媽咪、
父母縱壞的蠱女兒，
而我竟是個
不食人間煙火、
多愁善感、
不甘寂寞、
度日如年的
過客！

2019 年初，終於刪除了她

21. Sound Sounds Slow

Translated, 27th July 2014

Look, look; seek, seek;
Cold, cold; grim, grim;
Sad, sad; dejected, dejected; tragic, tragic!
Under the sudden warmth in lingering chill,
I feel restless and unfixed.
A few cups of light wine
Can't resist the evening wind that rises quick.
Over me a wild goose flies,
What rends my heart
Are the old figures with whom I'd mixed.

Covering the ground, piles of yellow petals peak,
While shrivelling, withering,
Which no one at present would bother to pick.
Tarrying by the window,
Perhaps this lonely one won't last to see it turn dark.
The Tung Wood trees join forces with a drizzle,
In the twilight,
Drops, drops; tick, tick.
What comes next
The single word *misery* could never sum up!

Translated from lyrics by Li Qing-zhao (1084 - c. 1151),
one of the few woman poets in Chinese poetry.

Appendix

聲聲慢
Sound Sounds Slow

李清照（1084-1151）

尋尋覓覓，
冷冷清清，
悽悽慘慘戚戚。
乍暖還寒時候，
最難將息。
三杯兩盞淡酒，
怎敵他晚來風急？
雁過也，
正傷心，
卻是舊時相識。

滿地黃花堆積。
憔悴損，
如今有誰堪摘？
守著窗兒，
獨自怎生得黑？
梧桐更兼細雨，
到黃昏，
點點滴滴。
這次第，
怎一個愁字了得！

22. The Scent of Shadow

23ʳᵈ October 2014

Shadow? Was it a shadow
He saw a split second ago?
A glimpse of a tinge sailing swiftly across the floor:
A flap of the billowing curtain?
A flutter of the wings of a jackdaw?

Faint wisp of sweet shampoo,
Hint of perfumed soap,
Between hanging in or vanishing from the draught,
Just a whiff of forged air, perhaps.

A girl with short and wet hair
In her nightgown of light peach cotton
Beckons him at the doorway of his room.
In the mirror
He finds himself a twenty-year old.

He follows her to the back stair of the hall,
Sitting by her on the landing to the roof.
The moment she tells him her name
He says "Oh!"
So unforgettable!

These are the days

Youth is an hourly gift renewed by heaven,
Spurting incessantly
Like doves and handkerchiefs
Flowing out from a magician's sleeves.

She closes her eyes,
Allowing him to lift her gown
To marvel at her snowy white thighs,
Glance at whatever uplifts him.
He touches her full round breasts,
She blushes, smiles, droops her head.

Shadow, a shadow,
He never sees her during daytime,
There are nights of her absence.
He wonders if she is a real person,
Could she be just his concoction?

These are the days
He relishes any girl's every single phrase,
Appreciating their every movement
Featuring slim legs,
Tapering calves, elegant waists,
Curvaceous hips,
Voluptuous breasts.

At other times they occupy the table
Next to the balcony in the lounge.
She does her calculations,
He adds up his arithmetic of musical notes,

Smiling at each other but saying no words.

Their back stair rendezvous recurs at times.
Women's bodies are sacred
For they'll give birth to lives.
Sex in these days
Cannot be further away from what he wishes.

Romance is no more than
The confession of admiration,
Light kisses on the cheeks,
Gentle and noble touches,
A passionate embrace.

Deep in the sleepless nights,
He is restless,
Bulging, dreaming of lovemaking
But settles for onanism.

One night he sneaks into her room,
Burying his nose in her neck,
Sniffing her bodily balm,
Sleeping with her in a light cuddle.

Dare not think of sex,
For he doesn't deserve her,
As he doesn't deserve
All the other girls he comes across.

When he wakes up she has gone,

As if she has never been there,
Leaving behind the shade of her smell,
Intended to be a keepsake.

Shadow, like a shadow
Was how you came and went.
How can I ever lose your name or scent?
You shadow, shadow!

23. A Journey of Breathing

25th October 2014

I seat myself straight and upright,
Legs horizontally entwined,
Open palms resting on my knees,
Fingers relaxing at ease.

I close my eyes calmly,
Getting ready to start my journey,
Thinking of nothing but my breathing,
Allowing the intake go through my nose,
Allowing the process deepen and lengthen.

As the cool fresh air flows into me
I imagine a flock of innocent lambs
Leisurely ambling through a gate.
My belly swells and rises,
Pushing my chest to open wide,
Raising my shoulders up and high.

Hold it there!
At least for a second or so:
Feel the sensation of your torso in bloom
As rotund as a plump sheep,
As full as a balloon.

After a spell of freezing still,
I allow the air to slip out
Smoothly, quietly, gently,
Until my belly depresses
As if it has emptied itself.

I might sustain the moment
Before inhalation resumes.
Then air again fills my lungs.
The energy it carries
Reaches every single corner of my body.

By allowing the cycles to come and go,
I hope to reduce the world's troubles
To a simple purpose:
Inhale and hold,
Exhale and hold.
Inhale, hold,
Exhale, hold,
Inhale,
Exhale,
In, go,
In,
Go.

We live in a world of air and energy,
Every emotion is in fact a mode of breathing,
Be it despondence, poignancy, jealousy or regret,
Be it fear, worry, anger, grief or impatience.
Re-programming our breaths is the first step

Towards the removal of the emotional trap;
Only self-cultivation is the ultimate key
To the generation of positive energy.

As the in-go process is moving on
I pray to the cosmos of air and energy:
Please guide me to lower my ego,
Free me from jealousy, lust, fear, anger and greed,
Let resentment and hatred unravel,
Leave my body to drift away.
Lead me to forgive and forget,
Let the emotional debts be written out.
We are doing these not just for ourselves,
But for everyone around us.

Please help those who need help,
Bless those who are ill.
Please enlighten the racists,
Help them to bring the world to peace.
Please allow none of my words to hurt,
None of my acts distress.
Please fill me with love and patience,
Let my sincerity inspire everyone.

By allowing the cycles to come and go,
I hope to reduce the world's troubles
To a simple purpose:
Inhale and hold,
Exhale and hold.
Inhale, hold,

Exhale, hold,
Inhale,
Exhale,
In, go,
In,
Go,
I
n,
g
o.

24. Roy the Painter-cum-Dancer

4th May 2011

Once below a time
The peaks are red, the ridges yellow,
A mirror emerging behind a jawbone
Amidst the cans, mugs and glasses in the cwm.

He draws as quietly as he talks,
Listening and observing in silence,
Keeping his own speech
Unspoken under and behind his beard.

He dances as calmly as he paints,
Turning a blind ear to the Master's complaints.
He casts, turns, dabbles and reels,
Following Jenni at her heels.

"Darling, this way," she pulls him and says,
"Make the double figure of eight.
Go ahead now,
Avoid stepping on Sau."

He spins with Glynis, the tall and proud girl,
Whose man Terry is the bravest boy of the world.

Here comes a Hay with Jenni and Janet,
Before joining the circle with Amy, Leslie and Annette.
His dance is graceful but his colours bold,
His brushes dynamic and powerful.
His lemon won't perish,
His jaw won't drop, dislocate or shatter,
His *vanitas* shall persist and last.

Roy fills every stroke with honour,
To invent a Pen-y-Fan of his calibre.
In a left-hand star he lives and rolls,
Where left is right and right is wrong.

Pen-y-Fan is the highest mountain in south Wales;
Cwm is "valley" in Welsh.

25. Bell Rings in Rain

Translated, 30th July 2014

Cicada sounds poignant in cold,
We face the long, dark pavilion,
The shower begins to halt.
Limply drinking the farewell wine,
The moment I linger,
My boat urges me to depart.
Hands held, staring into each other's tearful eyes,
Despite myself, words choked.
I picture a thousand miles of waves and smoke,
Rising across the infinite southern sky is the heavy
  evening mist.

Sentimental partings always deeply bite,
And are worse,
When autumn is chilly and bleak.
Where shall I wake up from my drunkenness tonight?
On a willowy shore,
In dawn breezes, under the dying moonlight?
This trip will last a year,
I shall miss all the seasons sweet.
Perhaps a thousand words of love may come up,
Don't know to whom shall I speak.

Translated from lyrics by Liu Yong (c. 987- c. 1053).

Appendix

雨霖鈴
Bell Rings in Rains

柳永 (約 987-1053)

寒蟬淒切，
對長亭晚，
驟雨初歇。
都門帳飲無緒，
留戀處，
蘭舟催發。
執手相看淚眼，
竟無語凝咽。
念去去千里煙波，
暮靄沉沉楚天闊。

多情自古傷離別，
更那堪，
冷落清秋節。
今宵酒醒何處？
楊柳岸、
曉風殘月。
此去經年，
應是良辰好景虛設。
便縱有千種風情，
更與何人說？

26. 姬莉的生辰

2018 年 2 月 28 日，3 月 6 日

棄我去者，
是誰早已不再重要。
不棄我者，
也不全是肝膽相照。
遇到是非難辯，
我用沉默招架，
無理取鬧的，
報以微笑。
逆來順受，
祈願世界和平，
不僅是為糊口。

不離不棄的，
每晚不是緊抱著我
就是想把我從牀推到地上！
不大不細、
忽大忽細、
二八年華的小寶貝，
說我是她摯友，
每叫一聲媽咪，
甚麼委屈都拋到腦後。

陶醉於她的
婀娜多姿、
千嬌百媚，
我每天活在二十五歲！

27. Tea Dance at Upper Chapel

23rd August 2013, revised 1st August 2014

On one of these gorgeous late summer nights,
We drive in a convoy under the light of a full moon,
Bidding farewell to the empty village hall,
Carrying home sweet memories
Of the enjoyment of our second life.

These finest days of our second life,
Are for merrymaking and laughter,
Reflecting on our past and present,
Forgiving the lapses of others
For loving and caring for our partners.

These best days of our second life
Will extend to years and decades,
Stretching ahead to beyond time,
But always staying with us,
Who shall remember your elegant pace.

Three hundred and sixty days remain,
We long for the coming of that evening.
When that hour has arrived,
We will drive through the villages
Heading for that gathering place.

We shall curtsy and bow to one another
On Upper Chapel's dance floor.
We intrepid naive toddlers
Will smooth out our best clothes,
Touch up our silvery hair.

Lining up face to face,
Bursting at the seams with excitement,
We await the grand cue from the solemn Master.
Some might greet his amusing grumbles
With childish little giggles.

28. Beth in A Nutshell

27th September 2014

Not a bit troubled by any feeling
Of humility or condescending
When offering food and drinks
To the folks of her home village,
At Strand,
Where she works
Every Saturday evening,
With her graciousness
And charming finesse
Which enchants the café,
And brightens everyone coming in,
Is Beth,
The seventeen-year-old girl
Who was born and raised
In Talgarth,
From where,
One day,
She will set off
To embark on her journey
To reach the world,
Which undoubtedly
Belongs to her
As she is striving
For brilliance

And every day blossoming,
Not just in her intelligence,
But as well in her passion,
Wisdom,
Elegance.

29. In Retrospect

31st October 2014

When being hit by cruelty of pain
The 17-year-old is just a baby
To relish being touched
She's an adolescent

Her grievances against her life
Let tears wash away
Unreservedly she cries
Quietly she sobs

Heading towards home
Sitting in a coach
She finds herself
All of a sudden

And love is all about
That's what romance, youth
Never doubts where it'll go
She grasps and enjoys the process

She indulges in love
On the last night of her stay
Excessively from dawn to dusk
Every day she grins and laughs

Will never leave the horizon
As if the sun
Of the stars and earth
As if it is the birth

Of weeks of thinking of him
Firmly grips the reaping
She hugs and kisses the one
Then the moment comes

Providing her company
For hopes are with her
She doesn't feel lonely
Alone in the coach*

*Retrospection starts from here.

30. Get Ready for a Pull

Translated, 7th October 2014,

Don't you see Yellow River's water pouring down from
  Heaven
Rushing towards the ocean and never returning?
Can't you imagine rich people saddened by their grey
  hair
Because what was dark at dawn is whitening at dusk?
Enjoy to the utmost when we're in celebration of our
  prime,
Never allow the golden cup to idle under the moon.
My heavenly-bestowed talent will some day prove its
  worth,
Re-joining me will be my dissipated thousand pieces of
  gold.
The butchered bull and lamb stew are for our enjoyment,
Should we drink, we must toast three hundred rounds.
My honourable Master,
You, young gentleman,
Get ready for a pull,
No more hesitation!

I'll sing a song for you,
Please prick up your ears.
"Precious dishes? Bells and drums? None is my

preference.
What I want is to rest in eternal drunken peace!
The sages since antiquity lived in obscurity,
Because posterity only heeds the names of those who
carouse."
The Poet Prince of Chen gave banquets centuries ago,
Where his ordinary plonk brought about the same fun.
Now as your host why should money worry me?
I'll sell everything to buy wine for us to share.
My rare horse,
That exquisite fur coat,
My boy will cash in them for booze,
With which we will redeem a myriad years of sorrow!

Translated from lyrics by the great poet Li Bai (701-762) of Tang
Dynasty.

Appendix

將進酒
Get Ready for a Pull

李白（701-762）

君不見黃河之水天上來，
奔流到海不復回？
君不見高堂明鏡悲白髮，
朝如青絲暮成雪？
人生得意須盡歡，
莫使金樽空對月。
天生我材必有用，
千金散盡還復來。
烹羊宰牛且為樂，
會須一飲三百杯。
岑夫子，
丹丘生，
將進酒，
杯莫停。

與君歌一曲，
請君為我傾耳聽。
「鐘鼓饌玉不足貴，
但願長醉不用醒。
古來聖賢皆寂寞，
唯有飲者留其名。」

陳王昔時宴平樂，
斗酒十千恣歡謔。
主人何為言少錢，
徑須沽取對君酌。
五花馬，
千金裘，
呼兒將出換美酒，
與爾同銷萬古愁。

31. 終於見到妳

2018 年 2 月 10 日

終於見到了妳，
無風、無雨、是白天，
時空彷彿停頓，
萬語千言
咽於唇齒間。

二十多天不見，
音訊斷絕，
恍如隔世，
沒有一天不記掛著
妳的凌亂短髮。

纖柔的嬌軀，
略帶病容的花顏，
打量我的，
不就是美都目光？
還是林村迷惘？

曾答應妳今後只談公幹，
抱歉又問起小天使來，
見妳猶疑片刻，

不敢多說半句，
就讓感覺留在心裏。
灑脫地告別，
輕聲叫妳保重。

並非至死不渝的情，
更像是對母體的敬讚！
不可名狀的交往
是否必敗興收場？
曾幾何時，
妳噓寒問暖，
給我舒服感覺。
曾幾何時，
幼女的任性
遇上了幼子的執著。

當一切無法不終止時，
明白妳必有無奈。
毋忘初衷，
唔再自怨自艾，
就用君子、淑女的舉措
來告別那
曇花一現的互相傾慕！

發生的也可能只是南柯一夢；感恩多於憎恨

32. That Chinese Girl of Narberth

27th November 2012

That fourteen-year-old Chinese girl
Doesn't have a clue of any type
When people turn around to look at her
To find out the meaning of "to admire".

Ever lengthening is her dark soft hair,
Rippling in the wind and profusely entwined.
They are not just her "silks of anxiety,"
Through them life and hopes are verified.

She droops her head to hide her blushes,
Can't figure out why people stare.
A colour of purity they are after
For her cheeks paint a rosette when she feels shy.

Blossoming are her graceful breasts,
Brightening are her brown round eyes.
No one gazes at her with bad intent,
Simply marvels at how growth is glorified.

Ever stretching long are her slim legs,
Ever narrowing is her waistline.

Her Irish dancing cheers everyone up,
Her xylophone sings like a lark in the sky.

Ahead of her angels clear her way,
Over her shoulders sylphs dance and fly.
Satan and devils dare not stay,
Villains drop their evil plots and smile.

If every person deserves a poem,
Every day of her girlhood is worth a rhyme.
For it is only by her freshness
That pristine beauty is defined.

33. On Joan's Birthday

9th December 2012, revised 19th October 2014

Worldly arrogance never troubles
Joan the plump angel.
In her humble world of faith,
She loves, but also hates -
When people get in her way.

Overwhelmed by parental excess
Is Joan the chubby princess.
Deep in her blissful character
She struggles between an angel and her anger,
And suffers in the name of the Father.

Never light-hearted
Is Joan the over-weight girl.
For all her worries and efforts she has made,
She prays for harvest from the stock market,
And for a gain on foreign currency exchange.

Never stops desiring food
Is Joan the trencher-girl.
When everyone is about to finish,
She must order two additional dishes
To kick off her real meal.

Two hours beyond normal time
Is the watch on Joan's wrist.
Inside the unneeded bags she carries around
Are all the files of her clients.
In the confusion of her life,
She can't afford to take any chance.

Beloved by her family
Is Joan the persistent Crusader.
She climbs high to impress her brother,
Earns extra to make her dad happy,
Keeps her weight to please her mom.

Adored by all her confidantes
Is Joan their gregarious soul mate.
Touched by her blessed and graceful appearance,
There will come a day, they believe,
She'll put on a content and forgiving countenance.

34. Ken Bowen the Firewood Man

8th July 2012

Dauntlessly I walk my dear dogs,
As I did in my daring days.
Fearlessly I stride through my lovely life,
Heroically holding my cane in my hand,
Savouring every step I take.

Tiny Whitey nimbly leaps over the fence,
Grumpily, Fatty Blacky falls behind.
Run, gambol, together they go,
Once I've made the gate gaping wide,
When the last glow of the sun suddenly shines.

Summer this year is showery and sour,
But glorious is the green.
Happiness clings to my heart,
I relish every footprint I press,
Don't care if it is dry or damp.

As usual, when winter is ushered in,
I shall fetch firewood to the houses of my friends,
Share with them my smiles, wishes and warmth,
Deliver my best blessings
To drive away the cold that none of us deserve!

35. Jenni

July 2011

I wonder if Jenni gets to the sea
With her beloved Roy and Collin,
On a cool July day of summer,
To catch fresh breaths of ocean air.

Behind the clouds runs a golden gleam
Bringing out her motherly beam.
As she sings on the sands,
She holds both men by their hands.

"Leave our worries aside,
Drown them with our smiles.
Let the ebb and flow rinse our toes,
Let the sunlight cleanse our souls."

The steps of a minuet she treads,
As the breeze combs her silvery head.
Her long blue skirt flares
When she swirls like a little bird.

Jenni's promised to write a verse
To recount their joyful day to me.
There she muses,
Clinging to the painter and her boy,

In sweetness and love
That shall never be washed away.

One of my earliest English poems, inspired by the love among them.

36. 聾舞孃珍納

2012 年 7 月 26 日，2018 年 3 月 1 日

聽晒佢話啦，
周圍啲嘢照樣咁郁，
淨係粒聲唔出。
佢用兩隻腳板
去感受地下嘅脈搏，
跟住空氣嘅節奏
跳嚟跳去。

靜脈裏面流緊一隻天籟絕調，
驅使佢好快咁氹氹轉，
一執仔攣毛由額頭散左落嚟，
同單薄、半透明嘅連身裙
响風裏面一齊映嚟映去。

光，响絕對平和裏，
係幾咁燦爛；
熱，喺死寂裏面，
直情就係興奮。
佢踩住一陣暖嘅氣流，
又响空中翻身。

腦中諗住嘅
係自己養嘅騾仔同馬仔，
仲有大嘅、細嘅鸚鵡。
如果佢地冇音樂都跳到舞，
自己做乜都唔使伴奏。

咁樣，又再俾佢話事，
萬有引力都解甩埋添。
佢响個度離地跳起，
條女咁就飛走左囉！

當年 70 歲的 Janet，從細就聽唔到嘢，但舞姿依然好正。

37. Lonely Traveller

17th August 2014, revised 19th - 24th August 2014

Without your presence,
How can I bear home's stillness?
How can I overcome fitful reminiscence
Aroused by our household miscellanies?
I must set off on my own,
To head for life-changing destinations,
Let loneliness redeem bygone indiscretions.

A deserted road is a godsend
Where I try to stay ahead and behind no one.
Choosing a comfortable speed,
Casually I proceed
While thinking what is your time
And what you are doing at the moment.

The air's freshness and coolness,
Are precious and generous.
The sky and omnipresent silence,
Are gifts over exuberant.
As the greenery is receding,
Past events coming forward,
My mind goes backwards
Trying to unravel my thoughts.

When dusk approaches
Where shall I stop over
To add some lines
To my notebook of poetry?
A tearoom, on the wayside,
The blaze of a wood-fire!
Where the smell of embers lingers,
A cup of hot tea is soothing,
A scone with jam and cream is tempting,
The faraway hilly slopes are inspiring,
A pleasant welcome is enchanting.

I am yet greedy of an extra bonus:
The sight of a boy's fairness,
A quick glimpse of a girl's unearthly air,
Or the scene of baby birds shuddering
When pressing their mothers for food,
So as to keep me in touch
With the world's beauty and wonder.

Sometimes I believe
I am the lucky one.
Most of the time I quietly say
"Thank you for everything!"
Yet who will stand by me
Or to care what I've written?
Who will reach my deepest sentiments?
Every time I think of my past
I see myself a troublemaker
Unlucky, distrusted, scapegoated, mistaken,

But not totally innocent.

When the gilded twilight is gorgeously spectacular
I ponder over some impossible answers:
Does my life have a meaning?
If it has one, have I outlived it?
If time can reverse, could I do better?
Why are such pretty things lavished on me?
Do I have a mission to accomplish?

Without you around,
I remain a lonely traveller,
Trying to taste loneliness,
That bittersweet romantic flavour
Which fires my imaginative flair.
Whenever the sun is glowing vibrant,
Wherever the rains are rinsing the rainbow
How much I wish you are here,
To share with me all of these!

Written at Penygawse Tea Rooms and Guest House, Llandovery.

38. Nine Pounds Forty

13th August 2012

The moment you were gone with the train,
My heart started to sink.
I drove to town, parked the car,
Decided to dine while writing a poem.

Before my first idea or the meal arrived,
I recalled a friend's previous query
Which gave me food for thought:
Why are poems full of words?

Why poets compose poems?
Why they lavish words luxuriously?
It triggered in me an epiphany
Which inspired my little ditty:

A jacket potato cost me four pounds,
I disbursed another two fifty for a charity pony ride.
After my jog in Bailey Park,
I stopped by Cwmdu on the way home,
Paid one ninety at the café
For a pudding and a pot of tea.

I must also confess
I had bought a bottle of water for a quid.

So, dear Amy,
While you were away in Cardiff,
I had spent a total of nine pounds forty
On the twelfth day of August
In the year two thousand and twelve.

Oh! Pardon me
If my words are excessive!
Perhaps all poets should learn to abbreviate,
Especially on this reckoning day!
Perhaps I need to thank Christopher
For converting my melancholy to mirth.

39. Lorac's Rough Game

25th July - 1st August 2014

Lorac is a good lady
But fond of a rough game:
When I ask a question,
She looks at some other person,
As if she's heard a voice
Spoken by a wraith!

My greetings to her
Get a cursory glance in return.
To my wife's sweet smile
She turns a blind eye.

To Jenny and Roy
She warmly beams and bids them farewell,
To my wife and I,
She doesn't bother to say goodbye.

We don't have any choice
But must melt her with our bare hands!
Next time we visit her café,
We'll dance to her face,
Signalling to her
We deserve a friendly gaze.

Our antics will soften them,
Our smiles will change their names.
They'll no longer be Lorac
But become Carol right away.

To be read along with *Carol of Blaenavon*

40. Captain Morgan

26th October 2014

I always salute Captain Morgan
Whenever I encounter him
In the monthly poetry meeting
Or in the streets of Brecon.

He is in Patsy's Café, the Cathedral,
The Theatre, Pilgrim, Cinema
Or wherever he could be seen.
Once I even bumped into him on the towpath.

He impresses me with his clean shave,
While wearing a tie and a suit,
Carrying a few books
But caching a tome in his lower pocket.

But I never know in his eyes
Who I am. Does he see
A Gurkha private or a regular of Patsy's?
The chef of a Chinese takeaway or a poet-to-be?

As once a victim of racism
He is naturally an equalitarian.
Yet I sometimes wonder
If he is a Carol or Lorac?

One day he gives me a surprise,
Saying "How are you getting on, Sau?
"It's been almost seven years
"Since you've moved here from Hong Kong!"

Then I figure out
No matter how bland his face appears,
His memory is sharp and exact,
His mind crystal clear.

Thank you for having inspired me!
May you keep patrolling and guarding Brecon
With your signature pride,
While I'm waiting for that day to come.

41. 瑪利曼女生

2018 年 12 月 3 日

我喜歡看見十餘歲的女孩：
整潔、
得體、
窈窕。

我喜歡坐近任何一個：
安靜、
集中、
芬芳。

或許會偷偷注目：
精緻、
有禮、
自信。

被她的長髮吸引：
嬌柔、
嫵媚、
亮麗。

牽動我是她的

長腿、
纖腰、
曲線。

心神不定是因
雪膚、
冰肌、
玉骨。

有時與她搭訕：
溫柔、
文靜、
優雅。

每次我都獻上祝福：
追夢、
大學、
堅持。

我讚賞她的美態：
靦覥、
緋紅、
女兒。

不忘安慰她：
放心、

君子、
詩客。

原是英文，為 6 月 1 日在咖啡室巧遇的中五學生而寫，12 月 3 日
譯成中文。

42. Remarkable Episodes

27th September 2014

Dear Antonia,
The other night you asked me
Whether Amy and I are happy
With the way people have been treating us.
Here are some of the remarkable episodes
We've found enchanting or disheartening.

At a museum of local heritage
We chatted about British history,
Inevitably about the Opium Wars.
I was trying to offer a donation,
"Thank you, but you don't have to,"
Said the curator in a sincere tone,
"We British owe your people too much."

"Where do you put the oatmeal?"
I asked the manager of the superstore.
"I'm not sure if we ever sell it," he replied.
His assistant reinforced him, adding
"I haven't seen it for a while!"
And all this took place
Just minutes before I found it
On a shelf next to them.

Amy and I were outside Argos
Struggling with a bulky package.
While we clumsily tried to push it into our car
A young man came over to give us a hand.
His smile was most pleasant,
His manner polite and gentle.

I found a café
That is supposed to shut at four.
I wanted to take away a sandwich
At the time of three forty-five.
"We are done," said the woman.
Curiosity drove me to enquire
"What time do you close?"
Without looking at me
She remarked "Now!"

We were speaking Cantonese
At an alfresco tearoom.
A gentleman stopped in front of us
Praised us for speaking "good Welsh".
A long chat revealed him to be
A member of a choir
Singing pieces from all over the world.
At last he left in delight,
When I promised to find them
A few Chinese folk songs.

I asked for the *Artists and Writers Yearbook*,
The shop assistant responded

She had never heard of such a title.
I told her I had bought it
Several times in this same store,
She insisted there never was such a work.

We were waiting for a table
In a café thronged with folks.
A couple courteously waved at us,
Welcomed us to sit with them.
They asked us where we came from
And told us they had been to Hong Kong.

At a restaurant that served dinner,
For fifteen minutes we the starving two
Remained unnoticed by any waiters.
When we finally managed to bring one over,
He just told us what were off the menu,
Then left, and didn't return
Until another fifteen minutes had gone.

Nothing can outstrip the bartender's manner
When we once had tea with our tango teacher.
He kept his eyes away from us
But only talked to the local woman.
Intending to test his perseverance
We bade farewell to him before we left,
But he still saw no waving hands,
Heard none of our words
As if we were transparent.

Dear Antonia,
I hope this finds you as it leaves me.
We don't live for the rough people,
But appreciate the nice ones around us.
Yours ever, Sau.

43. Whisper

26th - 29th January 2015, revised 11th July 2016

You speak in a whisper
So habitual to you,
Your words are terse,
Their lightness weights a load
Of heartfelt care
About me, I know.

I used to live for someone
Who has now gone very far,
Hatred and jealousy
Ruling over her,
Indulging in an ego
Running out of control.

I have come to a point,
Mistaken, abandoned,
Made a scapegoat
By almost every soul
Including the one to whom
I have written many poems.

You weep as usual
Despite being a mother of two,
Despite countless times you have told

Your babies not to cry,
Even though you are still doing so,
Soothing beloved ones around you.

As I am saturated with sorrows,
Between real and unreal,
Hopeful and hopeless,
I wish I decompose,
My components scatter,
Shards of me roam.

44. Cindy Wearing Tattoos

13th January 2015

Cinderella is the mysterious lady
Who has to go home early.
Anastasia is the princess
Having lost her memory.
Alice has not just ambled in the wonderland
But is also the Diva in my story.

She wants me to guess
How old she is.
This quip brings me back
To my boyish past
When girls all asked
Their admirers to do that kind of duty.

A girl's stature varies every day,
So does her age,
Dangling and swinging
With her passions and fantasies.
At present she wants to be eighteen,
A moment later twenty-two sounds stylish.

She said she wears
Four tattoos on her body:
One on the wrist,

One on her lower shin.
She doesn't have to invite me
To guess where are the rest.

At the small of her back?
Straddling her breasts?
Gracing her hip?
Or adorning her tranquil belly?
And that kind of food for thought
Will drive many a boy crazy.

Anastasia and Alice are Cindy's middle names.

Appendix

Cindy on *Cindy Wearing Tattoos*

13th January 2015

With rosy cheeks and a smiling eye,
I thank you,
Feeling very flattered.
And whilst remaining impartial
seems impossible –
and unnecessary,
This poem is absolutely lovely,
I think.
I feel quite special
For having been granted the gift
Of your quill's attention.

In a few years,
When our many dreams come true –
They surely will –
I would love to get this poem
Printed and framed,
A powerful symbol
That I am sure to cherish for years ahead –
But also a writing that
I shall never tire of reading.

45. 髮

2018 年 3 月 16-29 日

長髮的女子令我注目，
髮愈長，
注目愈耐。
垂肩、及背、過腰，
每一絲是思緒的延伸，
引我細心解讀：

沐浴在甜蜜青春，
是一把濃密黑髮，
至少是對歲月的抗衡。
紮起的馬尾
是魅力束勢待發。
不為本色動容，
是驕傲得發亮的銀海。
深啡、散放，
難掩十五歲少女
初嘗色彩的興奮。
紅呀、綠呀、金呀
營造變幻莫測的野性，
那怕是自憐自怨、
狠心、敵視、

期盼更好明天，
或圖藉謊言扭轉乾坤！

我也被短髮女子吸引，
髮愈短，
愈驅策目光探射：
是不受束綁、
我行我素的決絕，
抑或是化繁為簡、
暫棄花月？

一頭亂髮也令我側目，
愈亂愈觸發我探索
那寂寞但渴求知音的呼喚，
那管是背著現世愈走愈遠。
永不忘懷是長、散、亂髮的她，
唸預科時的夢中人。

從來陽光是髮的美容師，
為她披上彩虹。
雨絲是蒼穹恩賜的甘露，
卸髮絲的濃妝為淡。
風添神來之筆，
把扣人心絃的每一絲鼓動。

受女子秀髮吸引，

與性無關，
出自誠心欣賞，
皆因賞心悅目。
長短、黑白、真假，
可在瞬間調換；
光、風、雨中，
呈現無限變數。

善變、貪靚、難辨，
原是上天為女性的設局，
髮是為她們創做、
不會被自私、貪婪、妒忌
糟蹋的真面目。

給金髮的 Po

46. Wesley

22nd November 2014

How he lived
remains in the darkness,
How he blew life into his works
Stays in the shade,
How life left his carnal self,
A mystery left to be unveiled.

A recluse refraining from social civilities,
Smiling at nobody
But only to the shadows,
Have I ever met you
At any spots on the Mid-Levels
Or along MacDonell Road?

How in the middle of those nights,
Ambling back and forth in those streets,
Up and down steep slopes and stairs,
Pitch dark alleys and mews and lanes
Where he uncovered brightness of his kind,
Where he blended loneliness into the dark
Where he found a water lily rising from nowhere.

At times he panicked because
A light bulb had burst in his flat,

At times passions could outpour
Driving people to leave him alone,
At times fearing the water in the sink
Or that bottle of Chinese ink
Would drown him alive.

At times he preferred liberation,
Even just for a moment
From his medication,
The only way he could see
What he usually couldn't,
What others had never dreamed of,
And to hear
What others believed to be nonsense,
And to bear
What others thought to be superfluous.

The world found in his eyes,
The life he fantasised
Might well be less unreal than ours.
Things unambiguously true
Are often unbearably crude and cruel.

Emotionally fulfilling
Must have been those moments
As if an explosion was sparked
When splashing ink
Onto the canvas,
Allowing colours
To inundate the paper.

Landscapes of the faraway ridges and spurs?
Longing to reach unreachable destinations?
The blurred and misty images
Perhaps render what he had discerned
Through his wistful and tearful eyes.

How subtle is the difference
Between those strokes from his fleshy finger tips
And the etching of his crisp nails
Through which he directly
Unleashed his intricate, delicate self.

Self-pitying as being barricaded indefinitely
By a thicket of trunks, boughs, branches?
By forlornness and friendlessness?
By being left uncared for?
Yet fighting lonelily for recognition
Like me, with bare hands?
There are his worlds seen from his shaft
Deeply sunk into the earth
Backdropped by a clear sky.

Then that day arrived at last:
Couldn't predict how far
Solitude and imprisonment would extend,
Envisioning himself embarking on a journey
Through a waterway weaving between
Islands on the passage to paradise.

Leaving queries unreplied,
Leaving his family to look at each other in sighs,
Leaving awe and puzzles to me, this stranger,
Who had tried to celebrate his own birthday
At the very hour of his demise.

From him some are pleased to see
Order and self-control in themselves.
Yet some feel regretful
For lacking his audacity,
For being left behind.

His lonely self might well be
Wandering about the lonely gallery,
Feeling proud of his creations left in display,
Lifting our hands to feel his strokes.
His shadow might remain in the darkness
Guiding us to join his spiritual odyssey
To leave this world and this carnal life
So often so dull and so dry.

In memory of Wesley Tongson, a schizophrenic who painted
powerfully with his bare hands and died on 16th July 2012 of
drowning in his bath tub, aged 54.

47. Emma of Honey

16th May 2015

Some say she is the prettiest
Gardener in the area,
The most unassuming
Owner of a diner,
Fluting with a quiet voice
That couldn't be softer.

Some say hers is the sweetest place
Where people rest,
Families reunite and kiss,
Strangers become friends,
Exchanging blessings
Offering best wishes.

It opens to a panoramic view,
An expanse of greenery,
Undulating meadows and fields,
Folds of mountains and hills,
Enlightening those
Who get caught at the crossroads.

Butterflies are dancing with the bees,
Mother blackbirds feeding babies,
Swallows gliding up and down,

Bringing food to their wide-mouthed kids,
Sparrows hopping about on your table,
Cheeky and nosing into what you eat.

Inside, the paintings are like windows
Through which we see sheep and cattle,
Her girls are mostly smileful,
Stylish, charming and helpful,
One or two might look grumpy,
But only occasionally.

I don't know what she believes –
The *Bible* or *The Origin of Species*?
Yet she appreciates people
No matter how they look and speak.
I can tell she reckons
We are created or evolved as equals.
In our world haunted by racism,
Honey is my sanctuary and she an angel.

Written five days before leaving Talgarth for Hong Kong.

48. Reading History

Translated, 2nd May 2015

Apes and men bade farewell and walked apart.
Only a few pieces of stone had been honed
During those days we were kids.
When were bronze and iron first put in the hearth?
No one can tell exactly,
Perhaps no more than several thousand years.
Since then men could hardly smile
As they started shooting at each other with bows and
　arrows,
Flooding the fields
All over with blood.

Having browsed once through it has turned my head
　white.
What's left are bobs and bits,
A few lines of ancient deeds.
The Five Kings, Three Emperors and tales of myth
Have cheated countless passers-by.
Who are the real heroes?
Those leaders of the common people
Who brandished their hatchets.
Hardly have I finished this song
Than the sun has brightened *Dong* – the East.

Translated from song lyrics set to the tune *Congratulations to the Bridegroom* by Chairman Mao Ze-dong (1893-1976), spring 1964; the time he survived an impeachment after the Great Leap Forward Movement of 1958, China recovering from the famine of 1960, operas with ghosts prohibited, China ready to explode its first atomic bomb (October), two years before the eruption of the Cultural Revolution. His name "Dong" means "east".

Appendix

賀新郎・讀史
Reading History

毛澤東（1893-1976）

人猿相揖別。
只幾個石頭磨過，
小兒時節。
銅鐵爐中翻火焰，
為問何時猜得，
不過幾千寒熱。
人世難逢開口笑，
上疆場彼此彎弓月。
流遍了，
郊原血。

一篇讀罷頭飛雪，
但記得斑斑點點，
幾行陳跡。
五帝三皇神聖事，
騙了無涯過客。
有多少風流人物？
盜跖莊屩流譽後，
更陳王奮起揮黃鉞，
歌未竟，
東方白。

49. 待放苗苗

2018 年 4 月 7 日

自從緣份放我進入你的生命，
經歷了潮夕的漲退，
曾因你的淘氣緊縐眉頭，
直至最近才決定把你擁抱。

每次看著我們的舊照，
我驚讚你長得何樣嫵媚。
無疑你是含苞待放的花蕾，
只待玄機助你開得燦爛。

我知道信任不能強求，
誰也不能繞路，
但請勿把我拒於門外，
因為毫厘之差可以拉開千里。

假若你認同我、相信我，
那便不要間斷與我往來，
那樣我可以給你更多，
一起探索這萬變的世界。

50. Scratch

17th September 2015

You once said you wanted to scratch my back
Throughout the rest of our lives;
I said I would keep combing your long hair
Even if they would all turn grey.

We used to invent jokes to amuse each other
Before we fell asleep together.
Every morning started with my wake-up kiss,
Every night ended with giggles and laughter.

Appreciating beautiful things,
We marvelled at stunning scenery,
Pointing to each other rainbows,
Believing they are witnesses of our love.

We strolled along quiet streets,
Ventured out into the darkest lanes,
Cherishing our sharing,
As if they would last forever.

You and I promised to each other
We would travel together
In our journey to the end
Of an endless romance.

Then peace gave way to upheavals,
Child-like hearts broken by mishaps,
Miscommunications magnified by foibles.
For them, I offer to you my sincere regrets.

After battles over battles,
I'm still the same child.
Could we start from scratch?
At least give it a try?

Written for our 15th anniversary that didn't exist.

51. Countdown

9th August 2015; revised 3rd July - 8th September 2016

Every day is a countdown,
So is every hour,
Every minute,
Alas, to the end
Of our love
That at its expiry
Will have lasted sixteen years
Since our fairy-tale wedding
When we promised to each other
We would travel together
In our journey
To the end
Of an endless
Romance.

There was once a time
She shed tears
Over the poems
I wrote for her,
Laughing at the jokes
I ad-libbed,
Forgetting all misgivings,
Regarding nothing as unforgivable
Until my words

Didn't mean anything any more,
As I was losing my worth,
She picking the differences
No matter how much we share,
Placing someone between us,
Estranging from me and from herself,
Becoming more strange
Than a stranger.

Some memories bring regrets,
Some reminiscence hurt,
Alas, I must dry my tears,
Looking into the eyes of destiny,
Accept the unacceptable,
Put behind moments bitter and sweet,
Forgiving the unforgivable,
Allow time heal the wound,
Forgetting the unforgettable,
Let renewed love melt the impasse,
Before I find a new path
Of unending
Passion.

For the 16th anniversary that didn't exist.

52. Things I can't do

9th July 2016

There are things I can't do:
Sitting on the bed,
Folding my washed clothes –
Shirts and trousers,
Socks, briefs, sweaters.
I rather they stay in the basket
Buried deep out of my way.

There are things I can no longer do:
Sitting on the sofa,
Switching on the telly,
Watching the news,
Movies and unsolved mysteries.
I rather stay out of the room,
Let memories and images fade.

There are things I can't do:
Facing the breakfast table,
Brewing a cup of tea,
Putting jam on a slice of bread,
Pouring soy milk on the cereal.
My sight freezes in the air,
No matter how hungry I am.

No task is too simple:
Just a look at the blue flowery tie
Is too difficult,
To say the least about birthday cards,
Books you bought me and our photos.
Should I put them over firewood,
Burn them in the stove?

There are things I can't do:
Holding Porky and Goosey,
Squeezing and kneading their bellies,
Pressing my nose on their noses,
Smacking their fleshy backs.
I rather they stay under the blanket
Making sweet dreams of their own.

Those things we used to do together
Are things I can't do
Without my heart sinking deep in a swamp,
My head spinning,
My mind throbs.

These are things I can't do
Without tears in my eyes,
Without thinking of you –
That you I have lost,
That you you have lost.

Written while staying at the Mid-Levels.

53. 不因我們不能

2018 年 5 月 1 日

五月的第一天，
又一個美景良辰，
勾起我們曾經一起哭、笑。

你會打個電話
或到我留連的地方嘛？
我會給你短訊
說我在想你們嗎？

她會寫個電郵
慰解她不想見的人？
我會否再做首詩
表達我記掛她？

我會否願意說句
令你雀躍的話？
你是否明白
我想你做些甚麼？

你們會否考量
為何朋友變成陌路？

我會否思索
你們如何失去專寵？

你會想知道、
我又會否想說
為何我要把你們
剔除於記憶、將來、當下？

不，你、我、她都不會，
不因我們不能，
只因我們不會。

54. Tears and Petals Rustle

Translated,
8th August 2014, revised 26th September 2014

A baby swallow flies into a grand lodge nook,
Empty and silent, under the trees' afternoon shade,
In the cool wind a woman bathes in a tub.
Playing with a white silk fan,
Her hand has a jade-like look.
Gradually she leans on her side,
Dozes off as if she'll never be provoked.
Who abruptly pushes the door outside the curtain
Causing my ascent to heaven interrupted?
It happens to be,
On the bamboos the wind has thumped!

The half blossoming pomegranate
Resembles a red handkerchief pleated up.
It awaits other wild flowers to wither
Before giving you company in the quiet.
Should you gaze closer at its prettiness,
Its fragrant heart shows layers of worries like a clump.
Fearing the west wind
Might strip it to a bald stalk.
By the time you come to see me,
We'll toast our wines,

But you won't bear to offer me a gentle stroke,
For the petals and my tears
Will both be rustling non-stop.

Translated from the lyrics set to the tune *Congratulations to the Bridegroom* by Su Shi (alias Su Dongpo, 1037-1101).

Appendix

賀新郎
Tears and Petals Rustle

蘇軾（1037-1101）

乳燕飛華屋。
悄無人、桐陰轉午，
晚涼新浴。
手弄生綃白團扇，
扇手一時似玉。
漸困倚、
孤眠清熟。
簾外誰來推繡戶，
枉教人，夢斷瑤臺曲。
又卻是，
風敲竹。

石榴半吐
紅巾蹙。
待浮花浪蕊都盡，
伴君幽獨。
穠豔一枝細看取，
芳心千重似束。
又恐被、
秋風驚綠。
若待得君來向此，

花前對酒，
不忍觸。
共粉淚，
兩簌簌。

55. Love Transcends Words

31st November 2014

For more than a week,
Terry has been sick.
One day Ethel takes Amy and I
To visit him in his ward.
He looks perfectly alright
Except his body is weak,
His voice muffled,
Hardly audible.

At the time he greets us
He's holding a catalogue.
"I like this velvet frock,"
He tells Ethel.
"Bring me my credit card,
I'll place an order
Here over the phone."

Ethel furrows her brow,
Showing a face full of doubt.
"I'm afraid these days," she admits,
"I'm not hearing very well."
Neither can Terry figure out
What Ethel has said.
He is a bit cross,

Holding his wife's hands,
Twice repeating his demand.

"Ah, yes!" - at last she seems to get it.
"With your good doctor
I just had a dialogue."
Terry is quite upset,
Knowing his wife is deaf.
He pouts his lips,
Grimaces like a child,
Slouches in his bed.

I sigh quietly:
How ironic life is!
Terry will be ninety-one,
Ethel is eighty-nine.
Every morning is a celebration
The moment they open their eyes
Seeing the better half
Still there on the other side.
Having been together
For nearly seventy years,
They have come to a point
Where they cannot even talk!

When it's time to leave
We put Ethel in a wheelchair.
Once we get to the ground floor
She tells us to pause.
"Let me switch on my hearing aid

Before I can speak."

Then it occurs to us
Her deafness was a pretence.
"It's not just the money," she explains,
"That poor phone operator,
Will be scared to death
Should he or she receive Terry's call,
Hearing his spooky voice!"

When we get to her house
We think she deserves some cheering up.
"You are not just clever,
But also a caring wife!"
"Oh, yes," she replies,
"I was a good driver
And have never been scared
During my whole life!"

56. Dear V

3rd April 2018; revised 18th April, 3rd May 2018

How are you getting on,
My lovely child?
Have you cleared
Your distressed mind?
Once again,
I'm sharing with you
My thoughts, though uninvited.

I am excited to know
A fine boy of your age
Wants you to be his date.
Your mom also told me
That'd brought you dismay.
But it's not a bad thing,
You should feel proud, not ashamed.

As you are growing up,
A girl as pretty as you
Will attract countless admiring eyes.
He is probably the first,
But not the last of this kind.

I am very pleased:
How wonderful it would be

To see you meeting him
In a rippling nice dress,
Perhaps wearing Diorissimo
For that extra flair.

However, I must say,
A sixteen-year-old
Should be making friends
Rather than expecting romance.
Cautiously observe the person
To see if he deserves you.
No one could be your beau
Without first being your good friend.

You and him are very different:
As boys easily become aggressive,
A girl's heart could be fragile.
Girls should better learn
How to protect themselves.
Don't send wrong signals
That might stir up an obsession.
A relationship that goes awry
Is equally disastrous
To both sides.

Letting your studies sacrifice
Is by no means wise.
Don't give up your dreams
Of going to medical school.
Making friends and discovering love

Is a lifelong process.
There is no shortcut,
Only patience and good luck.

Should you think he's the one,
Go ahead,
Relish dating, cherish him,
But put your feelings under control.
When things are not right,
Be brave to say No!
Share everything with your mom,
Trust her, be comfortable.

As you are reading this,
I imagine your cheeks blushing.
Please don't be mad at me
For intruding on your privacy.
However unbidden they might be,
These words carry my hopes
Together with my love.

As enough poems have been devoted,
Enough wishes have been sent,
As you are reluctant to treasure my role,
Alas, perhaps it's time
I should leave you alone
For a long, long time.

57. 晚安－母親節祝願

2018 年 5 月 9-11 日

好舒服啊！
好舒服啊！
我仰天低聲呼喊，
好舒服啊！

四肢敞開，
如奉獻到祭壇上，
一切都交託你，
無邊的力量。

你不是神，
但養我的神。
你不是鬼，
但詭秘深藏。

喜也好，
悲也好，
遇上了你，
寵辱皆忘，
化夢一場。

是也好，
非也好，
閉目微笑，
身體蜷曲，
恍回母胎。

好舒服啊！
感謝你，
望你保守眾生、
保守囡囡與媽咪，
也保守天下母親，
每晚一覺到天亮！

58. Friendlessness

27th April 2018

You told me they said
Back then I hadn't a single friend.

They've guessed even now
I am isolated all the same.

They, and you, said that out of sympathy
Or out of contempt?

You have asked me to promise
You're the one I'll never disown.

You said they had told you
Not to see me any more.

But they don't know me
Any more than you do.

That night you yelled at me
To leave you alone.

Yes, I have been losing friends
No matter how hard I tried.

And now I'm in the process of
Losing my dearest one.

If you intend to hate me
You wouldn't run out of reasons.

At times I feel despondent,
At times I feel useless.

Or at least I feel
They think friendless means useless.

Some committed crimes, others lied,
But I'm the one who gets the blame.

They are hiding the truth,
You dare not look into my eyes.

Wherever a whipping boy is needed,
I'll always be there on time.

These are the people
I once thought were my allies.

If this is the path I am supposed to tread,
I am curious of what the purpose is.

Thanks to those who choose to stay,
For you, I'll remain intrepid.

Saying that I am friendless or useless
Is a curse rather than fact.

In order to make it work
They know I must be told.

In order to disarm it
I'll not regret but work double hard.

Those that can easily be lost
Shouldn't be cherished after all.

59. Life

Translated;
Spring 1986; revised 7th May 2019

Gliding down the slope of the expansive sky,
I am a light-off meteor,
Bathing in darkness, rains and the chill,
Hurrying on my way to a gamble.
Let my projectile life falling like raindrops,
Stirring up a night-long mist over the lake.
Enough is enough,
Life is so short,
So brief, yet glamorous.

As if by chance, I won at times.
The Creator was appeased by His splendid plot.
Yet the days slipped away like a pin
Carrying a thread of fading vibrancy,
Amidst my ten fingers' rises and falls
The embroidery revealed my prejudiced sparks and
  gloom.
Whatever,
Life is so rapid,
So quick, yet tranquil.

From the poem *Sheng Ming* by the renowned contemporary poet
Zheng Chou-yu (b. 1933)

Appendix

生命
Life

鄭愁予（生於 1933 年）

滑落過長空的下坡，
我是熄了燈的流星，
正乘夜雨的微涼，
趕一程赴賭的路。
待投擲的生命如雨點，
在湖上激起一夜的迷霧。
夠了，
生命如此的短，
竟短得如次的華美！

偶然間，我是勝了，
造物自迷於錦繡的設局。
畢竟是日子如針，
曳著先濃後淡的彩線，
起落的十指之間，
反繡出我偏傲的明暗。
算了，
生命如此之速，
竟速得如此之寧靜！

60. 望

2014 年 10 月 28 日

望，
相像中。
重有三日，
兩日、一日。
期望。

見到了，
點頭一望，
待擦身而過，
背影，
一瞬追望。

歡迎各位，
第九週。
不便再望，
故意
看相反方向。

淺響輕笑，
一臉亮麗，
長髮金、啡、淺黃。

驚豔，
誰不想望？

前望，
失落。
重有五週，
三週、
兩週。

各位再會。
若妳走來道別，
我會凝望、
親妳臉、
送妳這首小唱。

61. Marymount Girl

2nd - 3rd June 2018

I like seeing any teenage girl:
Clean,
Decent,
Elegant.

I love sitting next to one:
Quiet,
Focused,
Redolent.

At times I steal glances at her:
Decorous,
Pert,
Confident.

I'm uplifted by her
Slim legs,
Trim waist,
Subtle curves.

I'm attracted to her long hair:
Feminine,
Charming,
Enchanting.

Feeling restless because of her
Frosty skin,
Icy flesh,
Jade bones.

Sometimes I talk to one:
Courteous,
Sweet-toned,
Gracious.

I always offer my best wishes:
Dreams,
Persistence,
University.

I often praise her beauty:
Blushing,
Bashful,
Virginal.

I also reassure her:
Don't worry,
No voyeur,
Poet.

To the long-haired student I met
On 1st June at Pacific Coffee.

62. Maybe I'm Still May

7th November 2014

Thank you for remembering me,
Thanks for asking for my help.
My emotions are going to spill over
For I've not been myself.

Ever since I got your mail
My heart's started to ripple.
There're thousands of words I could say,
Maybe some day you'll know.

Maybe I'm still May,
But it doesn't any more mean the same.
Maybe I'm still Anna,
But you and I have gone apart too far.

I already promised someone
A long, long time ago
To spend my life taking care of him
Grasping his hands as we grow old.

Please forgive me
If my heart looks too shallow.
It has got no more space
To take one more piece of load.

Perhaps adding a piece of feather
Is enough to make me crumble.
Miring me in our memories
Is making me vulnerable.

The past is heavy,
The present is touchy.
I have a good husband,
I love my children.

Please let me go,
Not that because I hate you,
For I'm no longer who I was,
As I'm about to overflow.

63. 天后、長平

2019 年 10 月 19 日

從不闔上的眼睛，
旁觀世態，
見滄海變桑田，
桑田變馬路，
行人腳下，
多少夢想埋藏，
泥土深處湮滅了
多少是非黑白。

摸得著、望得見的真實
變成迷信幻想。
夢想高中的癡情漢
真的一朝稱王。
歌舞演故事、
時勢造英雄，
煙霧迷漫，
風起雲湧。

既然崇禎皇復活了，
我想化身長平公主。
既然王公卿相重新歸班，

何以你動也不動？
在血流成河、
吶喊歌唱的年代，
請保守我們
毋懼風浪。

帝王將相才子佳人，
催淚的人性光輝，
天衣無縫，
起承轉合。
十指纖纖的解語花，
英姿煥發，
豔驚四座，
但寧死不屈。

既然崇禎皇復活了，
我想化身長平公主。
既然王公卿相重新歸班，
何以你動也不動？
在血流成河、
吶喊歌唱的年代，
請保守我們
毋懼風浪。

64. Ever and Ever

7th April 2018

Ever since I've been thrown into your life,
There have been ebbs and flows.
Often I've frowned on your mischiefs,
Only recently have I decided to embrace you.

Every time I review our old photos,
I'm amazed at how charmingly you've grown.
No doubt you're a budding flower,
Just waiting for the magic of your blossom.

Trust comes spontaneously, I know,
No one can ever force oneself through.
But please avoid distance between us,
Any tiny gap could evolve into a gorge.

Feel comfy to open yourself,
Should you find me worthy of your faith,
Then I could offer you more,
Together we explore this ever-changing world.

65. Not Because We Couldn't

1st May 2018

First of May,
Another brilliant day
Redolent of those we have shared.

Would you give me a call
Or show up where I am?
Would I send you a text
To say I'm thinking of you?

Would she write to the one
She has decided to ignore?
Would I do anything
To show how I miss her?

Am I willing to speak
A word that would please you?
Would you bother to find out
What I expect you to do?

Would you pause to consider
Why friends discard each other?
Would I spare a second to think
How you've lost my favour?

Do you want to know,
Or would I ever confess
Why you have been scrapped
From my past, present, future?

No, neither she, you nor me would,
Not that because we couldn't,
Simply because we wouldn't.

66. 再在稻香舉杯

2019 年 12 月 26 日

分袂的時候，
點頭、告別、
道謝、凝望，
似很久不會再遇上。

仰望的偶像，
自嘲是擱淺的錦鯉，
相比之下，
我是充滿缺點的失敗者。

你背著行囊三、四，
獨來獨往，
我瞻前顧後，
悲歡離合飽嚐。

若問我怎樣生存？
放下自己，
不對號入座，
珍惜彼此。

再在稻香舉杯，

恍如隔世，
無限唏噓、感慨，
上次見面是何時？

珍姐也失笑了，
是……抑或……
彷彿是昨天？
還是今天早上？

給 Fish

67. Wooing Song

September 2014

The
Pebble roads in town are
Flat and sturdy, the
Watermelons big and yummy.
Here comes a lassie,
Whose braids are lengthy,
Her eyes are most pretty.
If you want to marry,
Don't choose just anybody,
I want you to marry me.
Take your dowry,
Bring your sister,
Hop on a coach to get to me.

I am a farmer
Hardy and healthy,
My fields are full of barley.
Here are my parents,
And my little sisters,
Next door my grannies.
Come join our family,
Everyone will love you,
We shall live happily.
I won't give you much work,

Just a simple duty:
Every year bring me a baby!

Our children will be
Cute and chubby,
And go to school to study.
One day they'll leave us,
Travel to the city,
On their way to university.
They'll find a good way,
Soften the tyranny,
Build up our great country.
We'll vote freely,
Take part in the nation that
Belongs to everybody.

Originally a traditional wooing song of the Uygurs of China;
The first strophe is adapted and translated from Chinese;
The second and third newly written, specially for students
Who took part in the democratic campaign
In Hong Kong in September 2014;
Intended to be sung.

Appendix

達坂城的姑娘
That Girl of Dabancheng

王洛賓　（1913-1996）

達坂城的石路，
硬又平喲，
西瓜大又甜喲。
那裏有個姑娘，
辮子長喲，
兩個眼睛真漂亮。
如果你要嫁人，
不要嫁給別人，
一定要妳嫁給我。
帶著你的嫁妝，
領著你的妹妹，
趕上那馬車來！

Groping in Darkness: Between Talgarth and Hong Kong

Author: Sau Y. Chan
Editor: Martin Lai
Cover Design: Kaceyellow
Typesetting: Chi Kwan Cheung

Published by Manuscript Publishing Limited
Email: manuscriptpublish@gmail.com

Hong Kong Distribution:
SUP Publishing Logistics (HK) Limited
Taiwan Distribution:
Modern Professional Distribution Co., Ltd., (Mod.E)

First published in June 2020
ISBN: 978-988-74584-2-5
Price: HKD78 TWD 280 USD10 £8

Published and printed in Hong Kong